*Meet
Me
Halfway*

ISBN   0-935906-01-0

This book was written

For those who are Searching
For those who are Reaching
For those who are Holding
And especially
For those who are Remembering

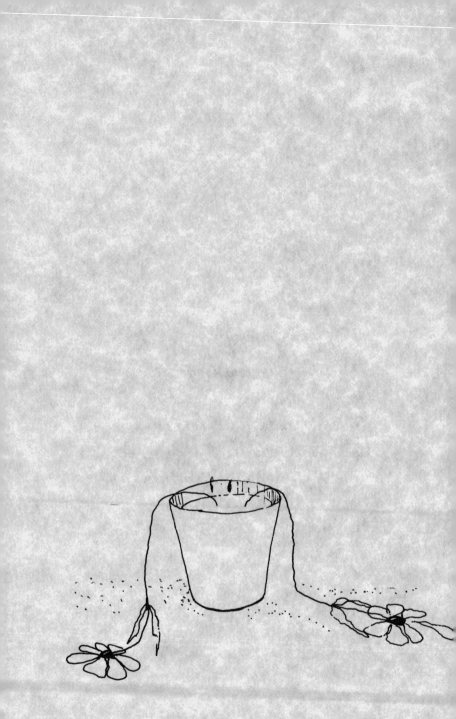

First, there must be a Need

All of us are born with the need to share
our lives with someone. During the years
the fulfillment of this need can be the cause
of constant concern and occasional pain.
For it can't be fulfilled by one person
reaching, but only when two are willing
to meet halfway.

I'm not asking
You to come to me
Only this
Meet me halfway

I've never met you
   And yet I know you
At least I know much about you
   I know you need food
      When you are hungry
   I know you need shelter
      To protect you from the elements
   I know you need things to do
      To keep you sane
   And I know that especially
      You need someone

I can't say that I am that Someone
   But I am Someone
      And if you choose to turn away
      Then I guess
         We'll just never know

Then comes an Attraction

A smile can open a heart
Quicker than a key
Can open a door

Fate determines
Who comes into our lives
Our attitudes and actions determine
Who stays in our lives

Today I passed you on the street
You gave a smile as our eyes did meet
In the rush of the day, there was only time
To take a picture within my mind
But later sometime at my apartment again
When the dark of the night and the lonelies set in
I'll flip the pages of my mind
And the picture of you I will find
Then through the night I will hold to you
A stranger that I never knew

And I can only hope that it might be
Someone, Somewhere
                    is holding me

Consider these two quotations

''Never speak to strangers''
''A stranger is just a friend
       I've yet to meet''

Which is more beautiful
Which is more often used

I didn't exist
    For a moment today
For when we passed
    You looked away
Not acknowledging my needs
    Or even my existence

But in the pain
    I realized
        How many times
            I've avoided eyes
That were reaching out—
        to me

Here I go again
  Reaching out again
    Probably, gonna get hurt again
    But at least I've got to try

For somehow it might be
That she has a need for me
And God, I've got to see
  Or else I'll never know

So here I go again
  Reaching out again
    One more time again
    But just a little more-
          tentatively

Love is an Opportunity
An Opportunity to give of one's self
And receive from another
An Opportunity for two
To equal one

And like all opportunities
We never know
When Love might come

So we must learn
Not to try to force it
But just to be ready
When it comes

We can only offer
    That which we have to give
We can't make others
    Accept it

In our language we have two words
    Solitude and Loneliness
Solitude is being alone
    Without thinking about being alone
While Loneliness is being alone
    And being aware that you're alone

One day as I walked
Alone in the park
Watching the ducks in the water
And the birds in the air
Enjoying the blissful solitude

I noticed a young couple
Walking together hand in hand
And when he stopped
And touched her face
Then kissed her gently

My solitude turned to loneliness

I've often wondered and racked my brain
But I guess I'll just never know
Why one person looks and sees the rain
While another is seeing a rainbow

We visit this world
For only a Moment
And that Moment
Is known as Life

During this time
We learn about laughter
But also of tears
We find more questions
Than we do answers
We experience the joy
Of new arrivals
And feel the sadness
Of loved ones departures

So we must try
To live every second
For oh, so quickly
Our Moment is gone

We are born into the World
Like a blank canvas
And each person that crosses our path
Takes up the brush
And makes his mark
Upon our surface

So it is that we develop

But we must realize there comes a day
That we must take up the brush
And finish the work
For only we can determine
If we are to be
Just another painting
Or a Masterpiece

The world does not expect us
To be more
Than we were created
Capable of being
But it does expect us to try
To be all
That we were created
Capable of being

I've learned
    That Life offers much more
    Than most people take

I've learned
    That many people live their life
        Within small circles
            Afraid to go out
            Afraid to let others in

And I've also learned
    That at the end of Life's game
        Most people wish
            That somehow
            They could have played it differently

Many people complain
  Life never gave them any chances

  We are given Life
  We must take the Chances

In every relationship
There's a chance of getting hurt
But once we've known the joy
of holding another close
We realize that it's a Chance

— We've just got to take

Based on Honesty

One night of sharing
Can produce a lifetime
of remembering

I reached out to you
Because I needed you
I will always remember you
Because you needed me

It's not so much a matter
of where we are
As it is
Who we're with

Nature gives us our needs
Society gives us our restrictions

In many cases
    Love that blooms quickly
    Like Spring's flowers
    Knows its season
        And then fades

    But love that grows slowly
    Like the tree
    Gets stronger and stronger
        As the years go by

    And yet the world
        Has a certain need
        For both the flower
        And the tree

It's not how long
   Two people have been together
It's how honest
   They have been with each other
      During the time
         They have been together

We must realize
That others exist for us
Primarily in our own minds
And what they are
Is what we interpret
Them to be

And in many cases
The qualities they possess
Are qualities we give to them

So when someone does not live up
To what we expect them to be
We should not only question them
But also our expectations

If I can not come to you
In complete honesty
Maybe I'd best
Just not come at all

It's a delicate situation
When two people come together
And one needs a friend
While the other needs a lover

And unless they have the wisdom
To communicate with each other
One will have no friend
The other will have no lover

It's not easy
To be honest
When you can use someone
To fulfill a need

In your eyes I can see
    Your need for me is different
       From my need for you
And the way I hold you
    Is different from
       The way you hold me

For while I come to you as a friend
You are reaching for a lover
    And this difference
       Can only cause pain

So when the phone rings
    And you find it's not me
And the knock at your door
    Happens less frequently

Please realize
    That a little pain today
    Is better than
       a lot of pain tomorrow

Love is beautiful
    When two people are sharing

But it is a tragedy
When one person is Giving
The other one Taking
And they think they are Sharing

I've often wondered
    Why I loved you
A love given
    With nothing in return
    But an occasional smile
        And a gentle word
    Enough to keep me hanging on
        Hoping that Love might grow

And I couldn't help but know
A feeling of relief
    When finally it was over

But now I frequently ask myself
Can something be over
    That never really began

We should do everything
Within reason
To save a good relationship
But if we are constantly
Trying to save it
It's probably
    Not a good relationship

I touched you
    And yet I didn't
I held you
    But there was no feeling
I knew your name
    But never knew you

Yet, when you walked away
    I felt a sadness
        For all the things
            That might have been

Some people say it as easily
As anything I've ever heard
But someday I hope, that they will learn
Love is more than a word

Love in our society
Does not work so well
Because so many people
Fall in love with the physical
Then try to accept
What's inside

When you fall in love
With what's inside a person
Accepting the physical
Becomes easy

Add Understanding

When you truly know the meaning
of the word Love
You will also know the meaning
of the word Pain

We can never know the true meaning
of other people's actions
We can only know their actions
as seen through our eyes

If you should try
   To understand me
      Through the eyes
         Of your experiences
Your only understanding
   Will be misunderstanding

For we have walked different paths
   And have known different fears
And that which brings you laughter
   Just might bring me tears

So if you can learn
   To accept me
      And the strange things
         I say and do

Maybe through your acceptance
   You will gain understanding

You have come into my life
    Through a door I was afraid
      Would never be open again
    For many have slammed it
      On their way out

So please feel free
    To stay as long as you like
But should the time come
    That you must leave
      Please, close the door gently
      As you go

There have been times
    When I needed you
        But you were not there
And a few times
    When you were there
        There was no need
But that's all over shadowed
    By the times I needed you

    And you were there

Pour on Affection

As I lay beside you
        And sleep has closed your eyes
        Our bodies still warm
            from the Loving
I reach out and touch your face
        Stroke your hair
        And once more
            kiss you gently

For in a world
        That seems intent
        On ``Making Love''
I find it necessary
        To spend a few moments
            ``Knowing Love''

Love will work
When the Lovers are willing to work
To make it work

If we must part
Then let's part with gentle words
Words like
''Thank you for the good times''
And
''May God go with you''

For in so doing
We not only protect
The precious memories that we've shared
But we also leave the door open
Should our circumstances ever change

Sometimes we have something
    Without truly knowing
        What we have

Sometimes we hold something
    Without knowing completely
        What we hold

Sometimes we are given something
    Without fully appreciating
        What we are given

But that knowledge usually comes
    When we realize
        What we have lost

I can live with the idea
That we are merely actors
Playing a part
But I do wish
Whoever is writing my script
Would learn to use
A few more Happy Endings

And a generous amount of Patience

Somehow
The conversation mentioned your name
And someone asked
If I knew you

Looking away
I thought of the times
I had held you -
Sharing your laughter
Knowing your tears
And then without explanation
You were gone

I looked back
To where they were waiting for an answer
And then said softly -
''Once . . .

I thought I did''

Someone remarked
That you had only
Brought me pain

I quickly corrected them
That you had only
Brought me joy

And it was the loss
Of this joy
That I interpreted
As pain

You gave of that
    Which you had to give
We learned to laugh
We learned to live

In my life
    Whatever it might be
I'll never forget
    What you gave to me

Artwork by
Harvey Wil▉

With a willingness-To Meet Halfway

Javan was born October 19, 1946, in a small North Carolina town. He lived in N.C. through High School and College, then moved to Atlanta in 1968. In 1979 Javan and his golden retriever, Brandon, started traveling around the United States introducing his first book to stores. He will be traveling at least another year, before building the home he has designed somewhere in the mountains.

During High School and College, he worked as a sales clerk in a department store. Also, he directed a day camp one summer and a Y.M.C.A. camp one summer. After college he worked as an agent for Eastern Airlines in Atlanta until 1977.

His main interests are traveling, all types of aviation, photography, and generally just about everything.

P.S. Javan is the author's given middle name. He pronounces it Je vahn.

I would like to thank the people who have taken the time to write. The comments and notes mean a lot to me. Unfortunately, traveling as I do my mail is held for awhile and then forwarded to me. It takes awhile to get, and even longer to answer. Some of the letters I wanted to respond to were lost. I would like to appologize to anyone who was expecting a reply and did not get it.

Sincerely,

Javan

"Footprints In The Mind" and "Meet Me Halfway"
are published and distributed by the:

Javan Press

% Champion Printing Corporation
      200 Fentress Blvd.
      Daytona Beach, Fla.   32014

This page is written especially
for those of you
who read the last page first.
If, by chance, this applies to you
then you have found a special book
that will be cherished many years.